Layla's
FORECAST
EXPECT TO GET DRENCHED

USA TODAY BESTSELLING AUTHOR
IVY SMOAK

This book is a work of fiction. Names, characters, places, and incidents are fictitious. Any resemblance to actual persons, living or dead, events, or locales is purely coincidental.

ISBN: 9798762468978

Copyright © 2015 by Ivy Smoak
All rights reserved

Cover design copyright © 2021 by Ivy Smoak

2021 First Edition

Chapter 1
LAYLA

I unlocked my mailbox and pulled out the mail. Bills, spam, bills, spam. I stopped in the middle of the staircase. There was an envelope from the National Weather Service. This was the third time that I'd applied for a job there. After two rejections, I was really hoping this was good news. I ran up the stairs and opened up the door to my apartment.

If it was another rejection, not knowing was better than knowing. I set the envelope down on the coffee table and sat down on the couch. The envelope stared back at me. It looked like the other two envelopes I had gotten from the National Weather Service. That probably wasn't good. If I had gotten the job, they probably would have called me. The envelope and I were having a stare down. It was winning.

I sighed and got off the couch. I poured myself a glass of wine and stared at the envelope from the kitchen. The first rejection I got was right after I graduated from college. They said I didn't have enough experience. It was disappointing, but it made sense. So I got a job at the local news station. I worked my way up to reporting the weather and then applied again. They said I wasn't a good fit for the position. That one didn't make sense. And it stung. I didn't want to report the weather in Miami forever. I wanted to make a difference. Wearing tight clothes and tons of makeup wasn't my idea of a fulfilling career.

I took a sip of wine. I thought I would have shaken this town right after graduating. I wanted to move north and experience what a real snow storm was like. And most importantly I wanted to stop working for Channel Nine News. They didn't take me seriously at all. A few months ago they had started making me do this ridiculous segment called Layla's Predictions, where I had to predict anything but the weather. It was such a joke. Maybe that's why the National Weather

Service didn't want me. They probably thought I was a joke too.

The envelope stared back at me from the other room. *No. This time is different. This time, I got it.* I took a deep breath, walked back into the living room, and picked up the envelope. *Please, please, please.* I slowly tore off the top of the envelope, pulled out the single sheet of paper, and unfolded it.

Miss Layla Torrez,

Thank you so much for your application for a position at the National Weather Service. Unfortunately, at this time, we have filled the position for which you applied. We were looking for someone with name recognition to lead...

I stopped reading. "Damn it," I mumbled, and tossed the sheet of paper on the coffee table. Maybe I should just try to get a position as a weather girl up north. If I landed a job in Philly, they'd have to notice me. I just needed to be in a bigger city. Nothing was keeping me here anyway. I had broken up with my ex over six months ago. I needed a change. I used to be adventurous. When had I become one of those people stuck in a terrible routine? I needed to say yes to the next opportunity that came my way.

Chapter 2
ETHAN

I clicked on the email that my boss, Cliff, had just sent me. It was actually addressed to the members of the board, but Cliff had copied me on it. After reading the first sentence, I froze. *That asshole.*

I stood up and peered around my cubicle toward Cliff's office. It was already empty. He didn't even have the nerve to send it while he was in the office because he knew I'd want to talk to him. Not that he was in the office that much anyway.

"Hey, Ethan," Bill said and plopped down in my seat. "Susan has her book club meeting tonight. Wanna go grab a drink?"

I didn't say anything. I should have known Cliff would put his name on my work. And he was lucky he wasn't here. If he was, I'd probably punch him in the face.

"You okay, man?"

"No, not really. Cliff took credit for the Blackstone Report. I spend four months researching and writing that thing, and then he just put his name on it before sending it to the board."

"Did you really not see that coming?"

"I guess I kind of did. I was just hoping that for once he wouldn't be a total asshole."

"Yeah right. So how about that drink? I can be your wingman."

"Yes to the drink. No to the wingman."

Bill stood up. "You've been single for six months. You have to get back out there."

"It's only been four months."

"Well, the two months you tried to make it work didn't really count. Madeline cheated on you. Done. There was nothing to work on. So it's been six months. Which means you need to move on."

I sighed. I knew Bill was right, but I didn't know where to begin. I had been dating Madeline since college. Just the thought of picking up a girl at a bar made me start to sweat. "I don't know, man. I guess I just don't know where to start."

"That's what we're going to do tonight. Come on, let's go." Bill started walking toward the elevator.

I didn't get to hang out with him as much now that he was married. Susan was great, but she always made him do super lame things. I was surprised he wasn't going to the all women's book club with her. I quickly caught up to him. I just needed to make him forget about being my wingman. "Let's focus on getting a drink."

"That doesn't take any focus."

"Right. I still can't believe that Cliff took credit for my idea."

"Let's drown your sorrows." He clapped me on the back as we stepped on the elevator.

***

"How about her?" Bill asked and nodded his head toward a blonde girl standing alone at the bar.

I took a sip of my beer. "Too blonde."

Bill laughed. "Too blonde, too thin, too short, too tall...what the hell, Ethan? Just go talk to one of them."

"None of them really seem like my type."

"Why, because they're not Madeline? Come on, man."

I looked up at the TV. Channel 9 News was on, but they were switching to the weather soon. Watching Layla Torrez's weather forecast had become a highlight of my days. A few seconds later she came onto the screen. Now *she* was the perfect woman. Her skin was perfectly tanned and she had dark brown eyes and long brunette hair. She always wore tight dresses that seemed to push her breasts up. And her smile made me smile.

"Oh, I see," Bill said.

"What?" I asked, without looking at him. My eyes were transfixed on Layla.

"No one here is good enough because you think you can score a girl like Layla Torrez."

"I didn't say that." But if a girl like her was here, I'd definitely try to talk to her.

"I hate to break it to you, Ethan, but you're not ready for a ten. How about you start with the seven at the end of the bar. Work your way up from there."

"That's okay," I said without even looking at who he was talking about.

"You're so lame. Susan will be home soon so I can't be here much longer. Talk to one girl. Now." Bill shoved me off the bar stool.

"Geez, fine." I looked around the small room. I hadn't had to use a pick up line in years. How had I first talked to Madeline? We were friends first. *I don't know.* I just wanted to go home.

"Now." Bill pushed my arm.

Fuck. I walked over to the girl that was too blonde. Despite what Bill said, too blonde was a thing. I just meant that she looked fake. She definitely wasn't a natural blonde. I stopped at her table and looked behind me.

"Get her number," Bill mouthed at me and pointed to his cell phone.

Ugh. I put my elbow on the table and smiled at her.

She immediately smiled back.

"There are two reasons why you should go on a date with me," I said.

"Is that so?"

"Mhm. Do you want to guess what they are?"

"You're handsome and endearing?"

"I was going to go with something more like no one will try to steal me from you and sometimes I can be pretty funny."

She laughed half heartedly.

"Was my line really that bad?"

"It wasn't great." She smiled. She seemed to like me making fun of myself more than my pick up line. Maybe I just needed a better line.

"Actually, you remind me of cheese," I said.

"Excuse me?"

"Because I want you on everything."

"I'm lactose intolerant." She grabbed her drink and walked away from me.

"Okay," I mumbled to myself.

"Dude, what the hell was that?" Bill walked up next to me.

"She just wasn't interested. I think she's a lesbian."

"You're such an idiot. Every girl that shoots you down isn't necessarily gay. She turned you down because you can't compare a girl to cheese and expect her to think it's a compliment."

"But cheese is amazing. I was being nice. Especially because that girl was anything but amazing. I'd choose cheese over her any day."

"Yeah, but girls are weird."

"How did you even hear me? Weren't you sitting over there a second ago? And you're supposed to be helping me, not insulting me. Besides, now I'm hungry. Let's go get some cheese steaks."

"Here." He grabbed my arm and pulled me back to the bar, toward the girl I assumed he said was a seven.

"Hey," he said to the girl. "This is my friend, Ethan. And ever since we got here, he hasn't stopped looking at you."

"Is that so?" She smiled at me.

"You're definitely the prettiest girl here," I said. I wasn't sure if that was true or not. I hadn't been looking.

Her face blushed.

"I actually have to get going," Bill said. "Will you take care of Ethan for me?"

"I think I can do that." She smiled at me again.

"Okay." Bill slapped my back. "Later, man."

All I wanted to do was leave too. I did want to get over Madeline, but I wasn't sure if this was the way to do it. I just needed to wait until I met the *right* girl. Not just any girl.

"So..." she said. "I'm Julie." She stuck her hand out to me.

"Nice to meet you, Julie."

She took a sip from her beer bottle. "You look like you're in really good shape. Do you work out a lot?"

That was worse than my cheese pick up line. "If you're asking if I can pick you up, I'm sure that I can."

She frowned. "Why wouldn't you be able to pick me up? I'm not like...huge or anything."

"Oh, no. You're not fat. That's not what I meant at all. It was just a pun on picking you up because of pick up lines." I laughed awkwardly.

"Okay." She looked embarrassed. I needed to make her laugh again.

"But speaking of working out. Did you know that every minute you kiss someone you lose almost three calories? Maybe we could burn some calories together?"

"Stop calling me fat. What is wrong with you?"

"I'm not calling you fat. I'm just..."

"Whatever, man." She grabbed her purse and fled the bar.

I sighed and sat back down at the bar. That was not great.

Chapter 3
LAYLA

"Do you want cheese on that?" said the man in the food truck.

"Yes," I said without hesitation. Saying yes to everything had made my whole day seem better. I had barely thought about getting rejected for a third time from the National Weather Service. I would have said yes to the food truck man either way though. Who wouldn't want cheese on a cheese steak? That was the most ridiculous thing I had ever heard.

I handed the man a ten dollar bill and grabbed my sandwich. If I really was serious about moving, Philly did seem like the perfect place. And they were supposed to have the best cheese steaks ever. I took a huge bite as I walked back toward the studio. Not that these weren't good. This cheese steak was amazing. I took another huge bite.

"There you are," Claire said and ran toward me. "I was looking all over for you. Did you hear back from the National Weather Service?"

I looked around to see if anyone from the news station was near us. I didn't want them to find out I was looking for other jobs, even if I hadn't gotten it. "Yeah. I didn't get it."

"What is wrong with them?"

I laughed.

"I really thought you'd get it this time."

"Thanks, Claire."

"So what was their lame excuse this time?"

"The said they had seen me reporting the weather and thought my make up was really horrible and they couldn't possible hire..."

"Shut up. They did not."

I laughed. Claire was my makeup artist for the show. And also one of my best friends.

"Of course they didn't say that. They just wanted someone with more name recognition. Which is crazy, because I assume I'd be working behind the scenes at a desk. A desk job sounds so good."

Claire laughed. "I don't think anyone has ever said that."

"Well it sounds good to me. I want to actually make a difference."

"I know. You'll get it next time."

"Maybe."

"Don't give up, Layla. You said they wanted name recognition? Then let's give them name recognition. You should start some social media sites." She pulled out her phone and typed my name into Google. "Oh my God."

"What?"

"Someone's already made a few accounts about you."

"What do you mean?" I grabbed her phone and clicked on the Twitter account with my name on it. There were tons of pictures of me on it, mostly zoomed up on my breasts. I hated Marty for making me wear such tight clothes. He was the worst producer ever. "Delete this." I pushed the phone back into her hand.

"I can't delete it. Once it's on the internet, it's permanent. How do you think Kim Kardashian became so popular? That sex video went viral. And now she's famous. Maybe this will help with your name recognition."

"But I don't want to go viral. Not for something like that. Maybe for accurately reporting a hurricane."

"Accurately reporting a hurricane doesn't exactly have what it takes to go viral, Layla. You should totally do something crazy when you're on the air."

"I'm not trying to get fired. That site is probably why I didn't get the National Weather Service job. They think I'm a joke."

"I'm sure that's not true. But really, I think my plan is pretty good."

"I already have to do tons of stupid stuff when I'm on the air. The whole Layla's Predictions segment is a joke. And I do that all the time."

"But it's not scandalous. You should do something scandalous."

"No." I bit my lip. *I'm supposed to be saying yes.* Maybe Claire was right. I needed to do something different if the National Weather Service was ever going to acknowledge me. And if I wanted to land a gig in a bigger city up north, I'd need to stand out too. "Okay, maybe." That was at least a little closer to a yes.

"Maybe? Wow. So what are you thinking? I got it!" she said as we opened the door to the studio. "You should do a nip slip!"

"I still want people to think I'm professional."

"Obviously we'd make it look like an accident."

"Let's think of something smaller. Oh, I know!" I snapped my fingers together. "I should just say something scandalous. Like let something slip about my political views. That would certainly get people talking."

"You're so lame."

Chapter 4
ETHAN

"How was last night?" Bill said and sat down across from me in the break room.

"It was fine." I took a bite of my turkey sandwich.

"Just fine?"

"Yup. How was Susan's book club? What were they reading?"

"I don't know what they were reading. But she definitely had too much wine. I got lucky last night."

"You took advantage of your drunk wife? Bill, I'm shocked."

"No. She gets super horny when she's drunk. She was basically begging for it."

"I didn't know that about Susan. Huh. I'm starting to see her in a whole new light. Good for you." I took another bite of my sandwich.

"I don't even know what you mean by that. But back to you. Did you get lucky last night?"

"Yes, actually. On my way home I found a heads up penny. And I got to make a wish. But I don't want to say anything else. Because if I tell you my wish, it won't come true."

"What the hell are you talking about? I mean did you get laid?"

"Laid? Oh, you're talking about Julie?"

"I don't know. Is that what the seven's name was?"

"Yes. Geez. You shouldn't refer to her that way. It's a little rude, Bill."

"So that's a yes? That's awesome. I didn't think you had it in you. She was pretty hot too. Does that mean you're finally over the dirty cheater?"

"I didn't sleep with Julie."

"What? Why? I set you up perfectly."

"I don't know. Our conversation didn't even last that long after you left."

"What did you do?"

I shrugged. "I called her fat or something. I don't know."

"Dude, why would you say she was fat?"

"I didn't. My pick up lines just went south."

"You're terrible at this."

"I'm out of practice. And I would have tried harder if I was actually attracted to her."

"You didn't have to marry her. You just need to get out of whatever this funk is that you're in. I'm sure Susan has a single friend she can set you up with."

"No, thank you."

"What's that supposed to mean?"

"It doesn't mean anything."

"My wife is smokin' hot, Ethan. You'd be lucky to land a girl like her."

"I know. I didn't mean anything by it. Obviously Susan is hot. Her ass is amazing."

"Okay, that's enough, smart ass. Don't talk about my wife like that." Bill loosened his tie.

"Calm down, man. Are you high or something?"

Bill laughed. "No. I was just trying to scare you. I was starting to think you didn't have any balls. Just wanted to see if there was any testosterone left in you or if Madeline took it all when she moved out."

"What, you wanted to see if I'd punch you in the face?"

Bill laughed again. "I wanted to see if you'd try to punch me in the face. Because obviously you couldn't actually. I'd totally beat your ass."

"Whatever. My balls are fine. I just want to move on in my own way. I don't need anyone's help. All I need help with is how I'm going to confront cunt-bag Cliff."

Bill laughed. "I like the new nickname. You should just be super passive aggressive. And definitely jizz in his coffee."

"Perfect. Operation Coffee Jizz. This day has new meaning."

Chapter 5
LAYLA

Claire put a few finishing touches on my makeup while Jack set up his tripod. We were going to broadcast a few yards away from the main walking path in the park adjacent to our studio. It wasn't overly crowded, so there wouldn't be too many pranksters making faces in the background, but there were enough people nearby so that I could pull one aside if I needed someone to interview.

"Any hints about what I'm guessing today?" I asked.

Jack shook his head. "I don't know why you insist on asking me that every week. My answer is always the same: I have no idea."

"What about you, Claire?"

"No idea. All Marty tells me is how he wants me to do your makeup."

Claire held up a mirror so that I could see my final look. I always loved the hair and makeup that Claire did for me. She was somehow able to tame my hair and make my pores disappear. But she had gone way too heavy with blue eye shadow and thick black eyeliner. *Oh my God, I look like a whore.* "Looks great as always. But can you get rid of a bit of the eye makeup?"

"Sorry, this is what Marty requested."

I sighed. *Of course it is.* I should have known that whore makeup was coming after I saw the outfit that had been chosen for me. It was a super tight, super short blue dress with a plunging neckline. And then they gave me six inch heels that looked like something straight out of a porno.

"Besides," Claire said. "This outfit is perfect for a nip slip."

"I said no to the nip slip."

She laughed. "I'm just saying."

Jack handed me a mic and an earpiece. I put the earpiece in and heard the familiar voice of our news anchor, Brian Scott.

"Our top story tonight is about the federal government shut down," said Brian in his fancy news anchor voice. "With republicans and democrats unable to agree on a budget, all federal agencies have been closed for the past week. But before we talk more about that, let's go to everyone's favorite segment where we prove that Layla can do way more than just predict the weather. Here are Layla's Predictions, sponsored by Sword Body Wash."

In the small display on Jack's camera, I could see the graphic for "Layla's Predictions" scrolling in front of clips from early shots of this ridiculous segment. First there was a clip of me trying to guess people's ages, sponsored by some anti aging cream. I got four out of five correct, but then some guy more ageless than Pharrell Williams tricked me into guessing he was at least twenty years younger than he actually was. As a result, he won a tub of anti-aging cream and I had to do the weather that evening in makeup that made me look like an old lady. After that I had to predict sports scores, stock prices, and what color car would drive by next. I kept hoping this segment would get canceled, but it had become quite popular and companies were paying more and more to be the sponsors.

"Now let's go live to Layla Torrez in Miami Gardens Park."

As Brian finished his sentence, Jack counted down from three and then gave me the thumbs up to let me know we were live. I took a deep breath and got ready to play. Even though I was a weather girl, I still got nervous every time I was live on the air. If I misspoke or did something embarrassing, everyone in the city would know about it. Sometimes I would watch horror videos online of broadcasters making ridiculous mistakes like dropping the F-bomb or that poor sports announcer who stumbled through an entire broadcast and then used the phrase, "Boom goes the dynamite." I couldn't imagine how I would ever recover if something like that happened to me.

"Layla, can you hear me?" asked Brian.

Crap, stop daydreaming. I put my finger up to my ear to pretend like my ear piece was malfunctioning. "Sorry, Brian. I'm here."

"Are you ready to make your predictions about everything other than the weather?"

"I suppose. What am I guessing today?"

"Penis sizes."

I laughed awkwardly. "Seriously, what am I guessing?"

"I'm serious. You're going to find guys in the park and ask if you can guess their penis size. If you guess correctly within one inch, you get to take their clothes and they have to walk home naked. But if you guess wrong, they get to take your clothes and walk you back to the studio to watch you present the weather while you're completely naked. They also win a bottle of Sword Body Wash just for participating."

What the hell? He can't be serious. Dressing up like an old lady and having to wear a Buffalo Bills jersey for 24 hours were one thing, but having to do the weather naked was in an entirely different category.

"We're going to take a quick commercial break, but stay tuned for Layla's Predictions!"

As soon as we were off air, I looked into the camera and said, "What the hell, Brian?"

"What's wrong? Let me just say, you look fantastic in that dress. But it's going to look even better on the studio floor. Or my bedroom floor. Either one."

What an ass. I was so tired of Brian thinking he could get in my pants just because he was the news anchor. "I'm not doing this. I'm leaving."

"I wouldn't recommend that. Before your time, we had a correspondent that walked out on a broadcast during a commercial break. Marty made sure that was the end of her career."

"So I have to stand here and measure a bunch of penises on live TV?"

"Guess so."

I pulled out my ear piece and turned to Claire. "What do you think?"

"I think it's perfect. So much better than a nip slip. Plus you don't have to worry about getting fired because this is what they want you to do."

"Claire. Please be serious for a second. You know I can't do this. Everyone will see me naked!"

"It's pretty ridiculous, but I'm sure it will all be blurred out. If anyone asks about it, just play it off as a joke and say the guys were clothed the whole time. Say it was a publicity stunt by Sword Body Wash. Everyone knows they have ridiculous commercials and would do anything to create a viral ad."

"But if I win, then the guys have to get naked. How could that be fake?"

"Like I said, it'll all be blurred out. You can just tell everyone that they were actually wearing tan underwear."

"And what if I lose and have to get naked?" I asked. The thought was horrifying. Only three people had ever seen me naked, and one of them was my doctor.

"Same thing. Just tell people you were wearing tan underwear."

"But you'll still see me naked. And Jack. And everyone in the park. And everyone in the studio." *Oh my God. That's so many people.*

"You better guess correctly then."

"I can't do this."

"Yes, you can. This is exactly the kind of name recognition the National Weather Service was talking about. So fingers crossed it does go viral!"

"Claire! This is absolutely not what they meant. This is a disaster."

One of our interns came sprinting down the path with a duffle bag over his shoulder.

"Hey, Tom," said Jack.

"Hi, sorry I'm late," replied the intern. "I almost forgot that I was supposed to bring you guys this stuff." He opened the bag and pulled out a bunch of bottles of body wash and a ruler decorated with the Sword logo. "Use this to measure, and be sure to give each contestant a bottle of Sword to thank them for participating."

I grabbed the ruler from him and he arranged the bottles so that they'd be visible in the shot. I was supposed to be saying yes. And in this case, I wasn't even sure I had a choice.

"Alright, we're live in three, two, one," said Jack.

Crap. Too late to run. I put my ear piece back in and prepared to be tortured.

"Welcome back to Channel Nine News," said Brian. "We're here with Layla Torrez to see if her powers of prediction include guessing penis sizes. Layla, are you ready to play?"

"I don't know, Brian. The park looks pretty empty. I'm not sure I'm going to be able to find any contestants."

"Nonsense," replied Brian. "How about that guy coming by just now?"

I turned around. Sure enough, a guy in black athletic shorts and a gray T-shirt was jogging by. *Damn it.* "Excuse me, sir, can I talk to you for a second?"

At first he didn't hear me, but then he slowed down and took his ear buds out. "Are you talking to me?"

"Yeah. I'm Layla Torrez from Channel Nine News." I pointed to the Channel Nine News logo on my microphone. "Would you mind if I interview you?"

"I'm on the news?" His eyes got big and he tried to fix his hair and wipe the sweat off his forehead.

Great. Not only do I have to measure a penis, but I have to measure a sweaty penis. "Yes. Can I have your name?"

"Mark."

"Hi, Mark. So today we're playing Layla's Predictions. Are you familiar with that?"

"Oh man, I love that segment. I knew I recognized you from somewhere. That was hilarious when you dressed up like an old lady to do the weather. What are you guessing today?"

"Penis sizes," I muttered.

"You're kidding," he said with a laugh. "You aren't even allowed to say that on air, are you?"

"I wish I was kidding, but I'm not. Do you want to hear the rules?"

"Sure."

"I'm going to guess your penis size, and then I'm going to measure it. If I guess wrong, then you get to take my clothes and come to the studio to watch me present the weather naked. But if I guess within one inch, I get to take your clothes. Either way, you win a bottle of Sword Body Wash from our fine sponsors."

"Wait, this is actually serious?"

"Yes."

"Will everyone see me?"

"No, you'll be blurred out." *I think.*

He shrugged. "Alright, I'll play. What's your guess?"

Crap, I hadn't thought about actually guessing. I thought back to my two ex-boyfriends. Erect they were probably five or six inches, but flaccid they were probably closer to three. I glanced at Mark to see if he was erect or not. He was staring directly at my cleavage, and through his athletic shorts I could see that he was starting to get hard. "Five inches." *God, please let that be right.*

"Alright, what now?" he asked.

"Drop your shorts."

He hesitated for a moment and then pushed down the elastic waist band of his shorts. His erection sprung up. It looked pretty average. Maybe my guess would be close.

I awkwardly held the ruler near his penis, trying my best not to touch it. My heart sank when I saw the reading on the ruler. Six and a half inches. *Shit.* Then I realized the ruler was backwards. I let out a sigh of relief as I flipped the ruler around and saw the new reading.

"Five and a half inches," I said. "Looks like I win."

"Hold on, it'll get longer," he said.

"Nice try, but the measurement was five and a half. You owe me your clothes. But look on the bright side, you still win a bottle of Sword Body Wash."

He reluctantly stepped out of his shorts and pulled his shirt over his head. I couldn't believe I was standing a foot away from a completely naked, erect man in the middle of a park on live TV. But I had to admit, it was kind of fun. *As long as I keep winning, this might not be so bad.*

I handed him a bottle of Sword. He grabbed it and immediately moved his hands to cover himself. Then he ran off.

"Way to go, Layla," said Brian in my ear piece. "One down, two to go. Do you see any other guys that could come play?"

Chapter 6
ETHAN

"Oh my God, he's actually drinking it," I said. Bill and I were standing in my cubicle, watching Cliff take a sip of the coffee we had switched out while he was in the bathroom.

"That's fucking disgusting," Bill said.

"I think he loves it."

"He's literally guzzling your cum right now. This is priceless. We need photo evidence of this."

"Absolutely." I pulled out my phone and snapped a picture. I looked at the picture I had just taken. Cliff was looking down at his coffee, frowning. I looked back up at him. He was staring directly at us.

"Shit. Let's get out of here," I said.

Bill and I ran into each other.

"That way man." I pointed to the elevator.

"Oh, fuck, Cliff's leaving his office."

"Go." I shoved him in the direction of the elevator. Bill hit the button and we quickly got on. The elevator doors closed before Cliff caught up to us. We both burst out laughing.

"Oh my God, do you think he knew?" Bill finally got out.

"I don't know. He didn't look super happy. Cum gets kind of clumpy in hot water, right?"

"Does it? Why do you know that?"

"You know, like when you skeet on a girl in the shower, it all clumps together."

"Oh, yeah. That's true. I didn't think of that. He probably got a huge chunk of your jizz."

We started laughing again as we walked outside.

"Do you think he's following us?" I asked.

"Let's cut through the park just in case."

"Good thinking." It was a perfect day for a walk in the park. A cool breeze was blowing in from the west that made it just cold enough so that I wouldn't sweat in my suit.

"I still can't believe Cliff took credit for the Blackstone Report," I said to Bill.

"Well, I think you successfully got him back. Besides, look on the bright side of things. Now that you're done with the Blackstone Report, you can finally..."

"Make myself a cheese steak. I know. I'm so excited. Or maybe I should make..."

"What? No," said Bill. "I was going to say you could finally go out and meet some girls. On your own. Without my help or meddling."

Why are we still talking about this? My failures last night should have been enough proof that I wasn't ready. "I think I'd rather just make myself a cheese steak."

"No. Not acceptable. You need to go out tonight and talk to some girls again. In fact, I expect you to meet one girl and send me her picture before the night is over."

"And if I don't?"

"I don't know. Maybe a rumor will start to spread around the office that you're gay."

"Dude, that's not cool at all."

Bill's phone buzzed and he looked down at the screen. "Shit, I forgot Susan was making an early dinner so that we can get set up for our Bachelor Finale viewing party. Gotta run."

"Speaking of not cool..."

"Only a cool guy would have helped you with Operation Coffee Jizz and you know it."

"Fair enough. But seriously, a Bachelor Finale viewing party?"

"It's actually a pretty good show once you get into it."

"If you tell the whole office I'm gay, I'll tell them you watch the Bachelor."

"Right, with my wife. Which is not weird at all. I'm just being a good husband."

Damn it, he's right. Bill jogged off back towards the office before I could stop him. *Would he really tell the whole office I was gay?* Knowing Bill, the answer was probably yes. *How am I going to find a girl to talk to? And more importantly, how am I going to take a picture to send to Bill without looking like a total creeper?*

Going to a bar seemed like the only option. Either that or just finding a picture online.

Then I rounded a bend in the path and found myself staring directly at a naked man streaking down the path. The guy saw me too, and before I could get a look at his face, he dove into a patch of bushes that looked a lot like poison ivy.

"What the hell?" I said to myself.

I peered into the bushes when I got a little closer, but there was no sign of the man. Maybe I just imagined it.

I continued walking down the path. It opened into a clearing where a camera man was interviewing a girl in a tiny blue dress. Her ass looked great. *Maybe I should snap a picture of her to send to Bill.*

Then she turned towards me and I saw that it was the smoking hot weather girl from Channel Nine. Layla Torrez. I always knew she was hot, but she looked even better in person. Her tits were pouring out of her dress and in those heels she had legs for days. And those luscious red lips...

"Excuse me," she said.

Oh shit, is she talking to me? I looked behind me to be sure I didn't make an idiot out of myself by answering her when she was talking to the person behind me. No one was there. "Hi," I said and walked towards her.

"I'm Layla Torrez with Channel Nine News. Can I interview you for a second?"

Yes! "Sure. I'm Ethan."

"Hi, Ethan. Are you familiar with Layla's Predictions?"

Hell yeah, I always watch that. "I think I've seen it once or twice."

"Great. Did you want to play?"

"What are you guessing?"

"Your penis size. If I guess within one inch, you have to get naked. But if I get it wrong, then I lose my clothes and you get to come watch me give the weather broadcast nude."

"So that explains the naked dude diving in the bushes."

Layla laughed. God, she looked sexy when she laughed. "Yes, that must have been Mark," she said.

Wait, did Layla really say she wanted to measure my penis? I couldn't have heard that right. "I'm sorry, what did you say you were trying to guess?"

"Your penis size."

"And my reward if you guess wrong?"

"You get to watch me do the weather naked. But if I guess correctly, then I get your clothes."

"Wow, okay."

"So you want to play?"

I took a deep breath. "Can you pinch me? This can't be real."

Layla laughed her alluring laugh again. "It's real. Are you going to play or not?"

And possibly see Layla Torrez naked? Hell yes. "Yeah, I'll play."

Chapter 7
LAYLA

I looked at Ethan and tried to size him up. He was taller than Mark, and definitely more handsome. He had a chiseled jaw that was already showing signs of a 5 o'clock shadow. The top button of his dress shirt was undone, and I could tell that he was muscular underneath his fitted suit. His smile made me blush. I realized that I was holding my breath while I looked at him. I gulped. How could I possibly tell how big he was? There was a slight bulge in his pants, and I realized that he was staring at me too.

"So what's your guess?" he said.

"Six inches."

He smiled. "Is that your final answer?"

Crap. Is he smiling because he knows I got it wrong? No, he wouldn't give me an opportunity to change my answer if he knew I was wrong. "Final answer."

"Okay." He put his hands behind his back.

I held the ruler up. "I need to measure."

"Go ahead. I'm not stopping you." His deep brown eyes dared me to undress him.

Challenge accepted. I reached out, unhooked his belt, and pulled it through his loops. Then I undid the button on his pants and tugged the zipper down. The fabric of his dress pants was taut from his erection trying to break free. He looked down at me and smiled as I pulled his pants and boxers down in one motion.

His massive erection swung out and nearly hit me. "Holy shit that's big," I muttered. *Oh my God, did I just say that on air? And even worse, is my guess going to be close enough?* He was way bigger than Mark.

I held the ruler near his penis. To increase the odds of my guess being correct, I didn't put the ruler all the way to the base of his penis. But it still measured in at nearly eight inches. I had never seen anything like it.

"So what's the verdict?" he asked.

"Eight inches," I sighed.

"Which I believe means I'm the winner."

"Yup, thanks for playing." I tossed him a bottle of Sword and turned to face the camera. "Okay, now we just need to find one more..."

"Hey, you said that if you guessed wrong, you'd get naked and I'd get to come watch you do the weather. Hand them over." He grinned at me and stuck his hand out. His penis was still hanging out of his pants.

"No, you must have misheard me."

"Those were the rules, Layla," said the overly excited voice of Brian in my ear.

"Alright, fine. Let's go back to the studio and I'll take my dress off," I said.

"No, I think the deal was that you'd get naked before returning to the studio," protested Ethan as he pulled his pants back up.

"It was," agreed Brian.

I could tell I wasn't going to win. But maybe if I took my dress off, they'd at least let me keep my underwear. I reached back, unzipped my dress, and pulled it over my head.

Oh my God. I'm in my underwear on live TV. At least I wore a nice bra and a matching thong. "There, happy?" I asked.

"That's a good start," said Ethan. "But you're not naked."

"Please don't make me do this," I begged.

"I'm sorry, but a deal's a deal."

You've got to be kidding me. "Alright, let's get this over with." I handed the mic to Ethan, turned away from the camera, unhooked my bra, and slid it off my shoulders. Then I slid my thong off. I covered myself with my hands and turned back to the camera. I was sure my face was bright red, but then again, I assumed no one would be looking at my face. This was, by far, the most embarrassing thing I had ever done. And I wasn't at all convinced that this would help me get a job at the National Weather Service. They'd probably blacklist me for life.

"Catch," said Ethan as he tossed the mic back to me. I instinctively reached up and grabbed it with one hand. As soon as I realized that I had left my breasts exposed, I brought my arm back down to cover them, but it was too late. I had already flashed Ethan, Claire, Jack, and everyone in the city watching the news. I was mortified.

"Alright, that's all for now from Layla. We'll hear from her again in a bit, but now we're going to move on to our main story..." I tuned Brian out and let out a sigh of relief.

"Alright, see you two back at the studio," said Jack as he loaded his camera equipment into the news van. Claire was already seated in the passenger seat. She gave me a thumbs up.

"We really can't come too?" I asked.

Jack shook his head. "Sorry. I wish I could take you, but you heard Brian. You have to walk through the park."

"But I'm naked!"

"I think that's kind of the whole point."

"Claire, don't you dare leave me here."

"This is what you need! See you back at the studio!" She closed the door before I could respond.

I decided to quit arguing with them. Maybe I could just run away rather than go back to the studio. I turned my attention to Ethan. "Can I have my clothes back now?"

"Sure," said Ethan as he bent down to pick up my dress and underwear.

Thank God.

Then he cocked his arm back as if he was going to throw them into a tree.

"Oh my God! Stop!"

"But I won them. I can do whatever I want with them."

"Please just give them back to me."

"I'll consider not tossing them into the tree as long as you agree to not cover yourself up any more. I think that's only fair since you got to see my penis."

"Not a chance."

He shrugged and tossed my thong into the tree. It caught on a branch twenty feet in the air.

"Okay, okay. Stop. What do I have to do?"

"Hands on your hips."

I moved my arm off my breasts and put my hand on my hip. My nipples were super hard from the cool breeze. *God this is embarrassing.*

"Other hand too."

"Really?"

"Yes."

I rolled my eyes and moved my other hand. Just then, I heard footsteps and voices approaching on the path. "Oh my God, people are coming. Please just give me my dress."

Ethan thought for a second. "Promise to take it off as soon as they pass?"

"Yes."

"And not cover yourself until I say you can?"

"Yes!"

"Okay. Deal." He smiled and tossed me the dress. I caught it and pulled it over my head as quickly as I could. I zipped up the back just as the group came into view. *Thank God.*

A few of the runners gave us funny looks when they noticed Ethan was holding a bra, but it was nothing compared to the looks we would have received if I had still been completely naked.

Ethan turned to me as soon as the runners had passed. "I'd like that dress back now."

I considered keeping it, but I felt like I owed him one after he gave it back so that the group of runners didn't see me naked. "Fine." I pulled it over my head and tossed it to him. I started to cover myself and then remembered the second part of the agreement. I put my hands on my hips like he wanted.

His eyes examined every inch of me, especially the parts that I had wanted to cover.

"Can we go back to the studio now?" I asked.

"Sure."

I took a few steps towards the path and nearly broke my ankle. I looked down at my heels. They had lots of straps and would be hard to get off. I tried to envision how to crouch or bend over to unstrap them without giving Ethan an even better view of my naked body than he already had, but such a task would be impossible. *The shoes will have to stay.*

"Here," said Ethan, holding his arm out for me.

"So you get me naked and then decide to be a gentleman?"

"Of course."

It was either take his arm or break my ankles, so I put my arm through his and we headed towards the studio.

Chapter 8
ETHAN

I had walked on that path many times before, but this was by far the best. I glanced down at Layla walking next to me. Her perfect double D tits jiggled with every step she took. It took all my will power to not reach over and squeeze them, but that will power was fading fast. To distract myself, I decided to start a conversation.

"So, what made you get into broadcasting?"

She looked up at me with her big brown eyes. "I was ten years old when Hurricane Andrew hit Florida. I remember hiding in my closet with my parents and thinking that I was going to die. And then the destruction afterwards. Houses were destroyed. Lives were lost. I was fortunate that my whole family survived, but I could just have easily lost my entire family or died myself. It might sound cheesy, but at that moment I decided that I wanted to do whatever I could to make sure that no little girl ever had to experience that. I had planned on working for the National Weather Service, but I couldn't get a job there. They said I didn't have enough experience yet. So instead I got a job as a weather girl. I didn't realize it would entail...this." She glanced down at her naked body.

For a second I felt a tinge of guilt for making her be naked, but then I looked at her and saw how perfect her body was. *Such a beautiful thing shouldn't be hidden under clothes.*

"What do you do?" she asked.

"My job title is technically Regional Brand Executive, but what that really translates to is me just doing all the grunt work that my boss doesn't want to do." I shook my head. "It's crazy how he makes ten times what I do and does one tenth of the work. And how he's allowed to yell at me, but if I say one thing to him, he can fire me."

"That sucks," she said. "But I bet he doesn't get to walk through the park with a naked girl on his arm."

Whoa. Is she actually enjoying being naked? "Speaking of my boss..." I pointed to Cliff as he rounded a bend in the path. He looked so pissed. He was definitely trying to find me.

"That's the asshole you were talking about?"

"Yeah. Here," I pushed Layla's dress towards her. "You probably want to put that on so he doesn't see you, right?"

She shrugged. "That depends. Would it make your day if he saw us walking together like this?"

"You've already made my day, but yes, it would be kind of fun."

"Alright then," she said, and handed the dress back to me.

"Hey Cliff," I said as we got closer. "Beautiful day for a walk, huh?"

He had been staring at Layla from the minute we came into his sight. "What the hell did you put..." his voice trailed off. "What the hell are you doing, Ethan?"

"Hi, I'm Layla, Ethan's girlfriend. It's a pleasure to meet you." Layla stepped forward and stuck out her hand.

"Hi," muttered Cliff. He looked absolutely shocked as he weakly shook her hand.

This is the best day of my life.

"I've heard so much about you," she continued. "You know, you and your wife should come to our place for dinner some time."

"I don't have a wife."

"Oh, I'm sorry. Well, we should really get going. I think the roast I put in the oven this morning is just about done and then I need to do Ethan's laundry. Ready to go, honey?"

"Yeah," I said. "See you tomorrow, Cliff."

Layla took my arm again and we continued down the path.

Chapter 9
LAYLA

My heart was beating so fast. I couldn't believe I just had a conversation with a stranger while I was completely naked.

"You're awesome," said Ethan.

I smiled. Even though it had been just about the most awkward thing ever, talking to his boss while being completely naked had been strangely exhilarating. And it made the handsome man next to me think that I was awesome. But I couldn't admit that to him. I figured I might be able to use it to my advantage. "Awesome enough for you to not make me walk through the lobby of the building?"

Ethan thought about it for a second. "You sure you don't want to? It seemed like you had fun talking to my boss."

"It wasn't that fun. And I won't ever see him again. I have to work with everyone in the studio every day."

"Okay, fine. I guess you've earned it. But won't you still have to broadcast the weather naked?"

"I might. But maybe I can convince my producer to let me broadcast alone from the old studio."

"Old studio?"

"Yeah. We had a new one built a few years ago. But the old studio is still there. They use it from time to time, but for the most part it's empty. I go there with some of the weather team when I want to do a practice run of the weather before the actual broadcast."

"Is it in this building?"

"Yeah. The staircase in the back leads right to it."

"I assume that's how you expect to get in the building without going through the lobby naked?"

"Well, you could always just give me my dress," I suggested.

"That doesn't sound very fun."

"Then yes, I'd very much like to use the back staircase. Is your boss always so angry?"

"No, he was particularly agitated today."

"Why is that?"

"That would be because I skeeted in his coffee."

I laughed and looked up at him. He was smiling, but he looked serious. "Wait, really?"

"He deserved it."

"Oh my God, can you do that to my producer? That would be hilarious. He deserves it too, I swear."

"I did not expect you to be this cool."

"What do you mean?" I was walking outside naked, but for some reason his words were what made me blush.

"Girls that look like you usually aren't so awesome."

"You just think I'm awesome because you've seen me naked."

"No, that's not it. I mean, don't get me wrong, you have an amazing body. You're beautiful. But you seem fun and down to earth."

I felt my face blush even more. I definitely never expected a guy to be analyzing my personality when I was completely naked. There was something extremely endearing about Ethan. It had been a long time since a guy had made me laugh.

We made it to the back staircase without any more awkward encounters. Ethan used the access card clipped to my dress to open the door and we made our way up to the third floor. I was glad that the staircase was wide enough for both of us. It would have been awkward to go single file and have Ethan staring at my ass the whole time.

I hit the light switch and brought the old studio to life. I always loved the old studio, especially now that it was always empty. There was something so peaceful about having such a big, fancy place all to myself. It reminded me of the old abandoned house that my friends and I would hang out at after school.

"Ever been here naked before?" asked Ethan.

"Never."

"Ever think you would be?"

I used to want to bring my ex here, but he thought it was childish. "Never."

"So how do you plan to talk your producer into letting you do the broadcast from here?" asked Ethan.

"I figured you'd ask him for me."

"I don't know. I think it would be super hot for you to do the weather completely naked in front of everyone. That would probably be the first time any weather girl has ever done that."

"Wouldn't you prefer if you were the only one who got to see me give the weather report naked?" I lightly touched his tie. "After all, everyone watching at home will see it blurred out."

Ethan considered it. "That would be fun, but I think the other would be better. Especially since you seem to really enjoy people seeing you naked."

Do I? Maybe I kind of do. "I really don't."

"Sorry, Layla, but a deal's a deal."

"Alright, fine. Can I at least practice my lines first?"

"Sure. That's what you said this room is for, didn't you?"

"Yeah. Okay, so here's how this works." I walked over to the teleprompter by the green screen. "Press this button here to start...wait a second. Want to play a game?" I had one final idea to try to get out of doing the weather report nude.

"Depends on the game."

"Sometimes we play a game here where everyone tries to distract whoever's reading. It's actually pretty good practice to get familiar with the lines and learn how to stay focused during the live broadcast."

"What do you do to distract each other?" asked Ethan.

"Pretty much anything. The only two rules are that you can't touch the other person with your hands and you can't obscure their view of the teleprompter. The winner is whoever can get the furthest into the broadcast without stumbling over a word or stopping."

"So I have to read the lines too?"

"Yeah. Part of the game."

"But you have so much more practice than me. That doesn't seem fair."

"Oh, come on. Anyone can read a teleprompter." *You don't stand a chance. It's harder than you think to read a teleprompter without missing a word.*

"Okay. Prepare to lose," he said.

"Don't you want to know what we're playing for?"

"I thought it was just for fun?"

"Not this time. If I win, you have to go talk my producer into letting me do the broadcast from here."

"And if I win?" he asked.

"Not going to happen."

Ethan laughed. "Okay, well on the off-chance that I do win, what do I get?"

"I'll do the broadcast in the real studio."

"You're going to have to give me more than that. If I just refuse to play then that would happen anyway."

"Fine. I'll give you my number."

"Deal. You read first."

I walked over in front of the green screen and took a deep breath. *This'll be easy.*

"Ready?" asked Ethan.

I nodded and he hit the button on the teleprompter. The words for tonight's broadcast began scrolling down the screen.

"Enjoy the nice weather while it lasts," I read, "because we're tracking some rain coming in from the west. It should start around 6 a.m.

LAYLA'S FORECAST

and then intensify throughout the morning commute, so be careful when you're driving out there, especially along I-95 between Naples and Miami. We're looking at a high of 68 in Miami, 67 in Ft. Myers, 68 in Naples..."

I looked at the camera feed to see where those cities were displayed on the green screen behind me. It was super weird seeing myself naked giving the weather report. *Stay focused.*

"The early morning rainstorm tomorrow should be all cleared up for the Dolphins game at 8 p.m. And with a high of 68, it should be a perfect evening for some great family fun at Sun Life Stadium."

Did I really just talk about family fun while doing the weather nude? And what is Ethan doing? I don't think he's even tried to distract me.

I continued to present the weather flawlessly for another thirty seconds. Then I saw a camera flash. I glanced away from the teleprompter as Ethan turned his phone so that I could see the screen. He had written out a text and was about to send the picture to someone. *And it won't be censored. Shit.* There was no way that wouldn't end up on that pervy Twitter account of me.

Chapter 10
ETHAN

My finger hovered above the send button. I re-read the message that I had typed out to Bill under the picture of Layla's beautiful body. "Ever watch the Channel Nine News?" *Bill is going to lose his mind. He's at home eating mangos and watching the Bachelor while I'm with Layla Torrez naked.*

"Stop!" screamed Layla.

I looked up and smiled. "I had a feeling that might work."

"That's not fair," she said. Her face was red. She looked so sexy when she got flustered. "You were supposed to make faces at me, not post nude pictures of me all over the internet."

"I was just sending them to my friend Bill. And if I recall correctly, the only two rules were that I couldn't touch you or obscure your view of the teleprompter."

Layla shrugged. "Fine. You're still not going to win."

"We'll see." I walked over to the green screen and Layla stood next to the teleprompter.

"Before we start," said Layla, "I think it's only fair if you get naked."

"And why would that be fair?"

"Because it's distracting to be naked. If I had to be naked during my turn, you should be naked during yours."

"I think you just want to see my penis again."

Layla bit her lip and raised one eyebrow. "Maybe I do."

Shit, she's good. This is going to be harder than I thought. I walked over to the old news desk and began disrobing. My suit jacket came first, then my tie, then my shirt. I could feel Layla's eyes on me.

"Keep going," she said.

I kicked my shoes off, pulled off my socks, and then unbuttoned my pants. Before letting them fall to the ground, I took a long look at Layla's body. I imagined squeezing her perfect tits and fucking her beautiful shaved pussy.

When I was nice and hard, I let my pants drop to the floor.

Holy shit. I'm naked with Layla Torrez. How is this happening?

"That's better," she said.

I walked back to the green screen and Layla hit the switch on the teleprompter.

"Enjoy the nice weather while it lasts, because we're tracking some rain coming in from the west. It should start around 6 a.m. and then intensify throughout the morning commute..."

As expected, Layla's first move was to grab my phone and take a picture of me. She pretended to send it to someone. Maybe she actually did. Her next move was equally predictable. She reached up and squeezed both of her tits while looking at me with sex eyes. *Holy shit that's hot.* Then she put her hands on the teleprompter, arched her back, and stuck her ass in the air.

I was tempted to stare at her perfectly round ass, but if I won this game and got her number then I might be able to eventually do more than just stare at it. I focused as hard as I could on the teleprompter and continued reading.

"The early morning rainstorm tomorrow should be all cleared up for the Dolphins game at 8 p.m."

I was getting close to where I had distracted her, and she was out of tricks. Or so I thought.

She calmly walked towards me, being careful not to block my view of the teleprompter. Then she dropped to her knees directly in front of me. My erection was no more than an inch or two away from her face. I stayed focused on the teleprompter but I could tell she was staring up at me with her big brown eyes and playing with her tits.

Don't look down, don't look down.

She leaned in and flicked her tongue against the tip of my erection.

Just a few more lines.

Her soft lips wrapped around my tip. They felt even better than I had imagined. I pushed my hips forward slightly and she leaned in to suck more of my cock. She continued swirling her tongue around as she leaned in further. She kept the pace nice and slow for a few seconds before speeding up.

I looked down and locked eyes with her as she bobbed up and down.

She pulled back and smiled. "Damn it. You got one line farther than me."

I looked up at the teleprompter. I didn't remember saying any of the lines that were showing, but I guess I had somehow managed to continue reading far enough to win. *I won! But I wish she would keep going.* "Why'd you stop?"

"Stop what?" She was now standing by the teleprompter with an innocent look on her face.

"Giving me head. And hey, wasn't that against the rules?"

"I don't know what you're talking about."

Chapter 11
LAYLA

"What do you mean? You definitely just gave me head," Ethan said.

"You have a pretty wild imagination. You may have gotten me naked within minutes of meeting me, but I would never give a stranger head." *Oh my God, I just gave a stranger head.*

He shook his head and looked frustrated. His expression was really hot. Or maybe it was just his body that was so hot. His torso was even more toned than I expected. I counted each muscle in his six pack and then followed the lines down to his huge erection. *Huge.* When I was sucking on it I could only fit a little over half of it in my mouth. *Maybe I should give in and keep going.*

My producer, Marty, burst in the door.

Even though it was against Ethan's rules, I covered myself with both hands. Having someone I knew see me naked was so much more awkward than a stranger seeing me. And it would be a million times worse when it was Brian. I would never hear the end of it from him.

"Layla...wow." Marty stopped and looked me up and down. "You're on in three minutes."

"Okay. I'm coming."

Marty kept his gaze on me for a minute and then left.

"Ready to go?" I asked Ethan.

"Sure, just let me grab my clothes."

"No way. If I'm going to do the weather report naked on live TV, the least you can do is stand in the studio naked with me."

"And why would I do that?"

I gave him my most seductive smile.

"Okay, I'll do it."

That was easy.

He walked over and offered me his muscular arm. His cock was still rock hard.

We paused outside the door to the main studio. I could hear my co-workers voices inside. *They're all about to see me naked. Not only that, but they're all going to see Ethan's erection. Oh God, will they know I just sucked it?*

Ethan turned to me and smiled.

For some reason his smile made me a little less nervous.

"You know, you remind me of cheese," he said.

I laughed. "Why is that, Ethan?"

"Because I want you on everything."

I starting laughing again. "At first I thought I should be insulted. But I really love cheese. I like it on everything too."

"You do?" He smiled at me.

"Who doesn't?" I asked. "My favorite food is cheese steaks."

"Me too! Those are the best."

"There's this food truck right outside that sells the best..."

"I go there all the time. I can't believe we haven't run into each other before."

"I would have remembered running into you," I said.

"I know why I'd remember running into you...because you're famous in Miami. But why would you remember running into me?" He flashed me a smile.

"What? I don't know what you're talking about. Why are we talking about cheese right now? You're making me hungry." He was sexy. Really sexy. And it was getting harder not to stare down at his erection.

He laughed. "I was just trying to make you less nervous. Here we go," said Ethan as he pushed the doors open. "Just pretend like you aren't naked."

Brian was in the middle of giving some report in his stupid news anchor voice, but he paused for a second and looked over. When he did, everyone in the studio followed his eyes to see where he was looking. I don't know how many people it was. Probably twenty or so.

I decided to follow Ethan's advice. I pulled him towards my makeup chair where Claire was waiting for me. It was refreshing to see her focus on Ethan's erection rather than my breasts.

I sat down and crossed my legs.

"Oh my God," Claire mouthed at me while she got to work on touching up my hair and makeup. She nodded toward Ethan's enormous cock.

"Stop it!" I mouthed back.

To try to relax, I started doing a few breathing exercises, but they were useless. My heart was beating faster and faster with every second that passed.

I looked up at the clock and saw that it was 5:39, which meant it was time for me to take my place in front of the green screen to ensure I would be ready to begin the weather report at 5:40. *Shit, this is really happening.*

"Good luck," whispered Ethan as I made my way to the green screen. "And good luck not being distracted," he added with a wink.

"You're not supposed to do that during the actual broadcast," I said.

Ethan pointed to his ear and mouthed "Sorry, didn't catch that."

He better be joking.

The lights were super bright and I couldn't help but notice the "HD" in big letters on the front of the camera. It was bad enough having people be able to see every little flaw on my face, but now they would get to see my naked body too. Sure, parts of me would be blurred out, but everyone would still see far more of me than they would if I was wearing a dress.

"And now let's take it over to Layla Torrez for the weather," said Brian.

A red light on the camera told me that I was live. Ethan was standing next to the camera giving me a thumbs up while Marty whispered something in his ear. Hopefully he was telling him not to distract me at all. Or maybe he was telling him to put his giant penis away.

"Thanks, Brian," I said. I was ready to read my first line, but it didn't appear on the teleprompter yet.

Brian started talking again. "So for those of you just tuning in, earlier on Layla's Predictions sponsored by Sword Body Wash, Layla had to try to guess penis sizes of men she had never met before. She got the first one right, but then she way underestimated the second one. As her punishment, she has to do the weather naked. How does it feel, Layla?"

"Oh, it's great," I said sarcastically. "It certainly made wardrobe selection easier."

"Maybe you should always dress like that."

"Tempting offer, but no thanks."

"Okay. Well, I'm sure our viewers are enjoying it."

"I certainly hope so. But I think that they'd appreciate it even more if I told them about the weather like I'm supposed to."

"Fair enough."

My lines appeared on the teleprompter. " Enjoy the nice weather while it lasts, because we're tracking some rain coming in from the west. It should start around 6 a.m. and then intensify throughout the morning commute, so be careful when you're driving out there, especially along I-95 between Naples and Miami. " I turned to the side and pointed at the green screen. *Great, now everyone gets the side view of me as well.*

When I turned back to look at the teleprompter, Ethan had disappeared.

"We're looking at a high of 68 in Miami, 67 in Ft. Myers..." On the camera feed I saw Ethan approach behind me, his huge erection still at full force. "...68 in Naples, and 73 down by the shore."

As I said the next line, Ethan reached around and grabbed my breasts. *What the fuck is he doing?! He can't feel me up on live TV.*

I focused on the teleprompter and continued, "The early morning rainstorm tomorrow should be all cleared up for the Dolphins game at 8 p.m."

Ethan's hands left my breasts and wandered down across my stomach. Then his hand went between my legs. *Oh my God.* He messaged my clit and slipped one of his fingers inside of me. I couldn't stop the moan that escaped from my lips. *This can't be happening.*

I glanced at Marty for a queue about what to do. His eyes were wide but he gave me the signal to keep talking. I figured they must have cut to a graphic as soon as they saw Ethan walk up behind me.

"And with a high of 68, it should be a perfect evening for some great family fun at Sun Life Stadium."

Ethan slid his hard cock across my ass until it was between my legs. *Fuck.* The tip of it pushed up against my clit. I was so wet. All I wanted to do was bend over and feel all eight inches of him inside of me. But I was in the middle of the studio doing a live broadcast to millions of people. I couldn't just bend over and let him fuck me. *Who am I kidding? Everyone in the studio has already seen him finger me. Why not just bend over and enjoy it?* My mind took back control from my hormones. *What am I thinking?! I can't do that.*

"For the 10 day forecast, we're predicting..." The words on the teleprompter seemed endless and all I wanted was for the broadcast to be over so that I could have Ethan's huge cock inside of me. I couldn't focus with him teasing me. I decided to cut the broadcast short. "We're predicting that it's going to be really hot all week. Back to you, Brian."

"Thanks, Layla," said Brian. "We'll be back after a quick message from our sponsors."

I turned to face Ethan. I couldn't decide if I should yell at him or suck his cock.

Before I could say anything, Marty walked up. Despite the fact that Ethan had just fingered me during the weather report, Marty had a huge smile on his face.

"I just heard from the Sword marketing rep," he said.

"I didn't know Ethan was going to..." I started, but Marty waved his hand to cut me off.

"No, that was awesome. I told him to do it. But Sword wants us to take it even further. They want Ethan to fuck you."

My jaw dropped. "What?"

"They want him to fuck you on live TV. And they're willing to pay us a ton to make it happen."

"Just because I'm naked doesn't mean I'm going to shoot a porno. Anyway, the FCC would never allow it."

"I don't know if you were listening to Brian's top story tonight, but the federal government shutdown means that all federal agencies are closed. That includes the FCC. We can show whatever we want."

"Including porn?"

"Yup. The preliminary numbers are showing that this is our highest rated broadcast ever. And that's just from showing your tits. Imagine..."

"Wait, they were censored, right?"

"Of course."

Thank God.

"It's your choice. But the station could really use the money that Sword is offering. It would definitely be enough to give the entire meteorology team a well deserved bonus."

"So I can say no?"

"Well, without that money we'll struggle to deal with all the complaints that we'll surely receive from showing your tits during primetime. Someone might get fired over the whole thing."

"Are you threatening to fire me?" I asked. This was completely unfair. *How will I ever get a job at the National Weather Service now?* I couldn't think straight with Ethan's huge erection next to me.

"No, that would not be appropriate. We're back on in a minute. I hope you make the right choice."

I walked back to the green screen and prepared for the broadcast to resume.

Chapter 12
ETHAN

I stood by the teleprompter and looked Layla's tan body up and down. Finally getting to grab her tits and feel her wet pussy had been incredible, but I hoped she would agree to take it further. Sure, it would be awkward doing it on live TV, but I was so horny that I didn't care. I would do anything to feel those soft lips on my cock again. And it was more than that. She liked my cheese pick up line. If there was ever a keeper, it was Layla Torrez. And I wasn't going to let her get away. I was going to seal the deal.

"Welcome back to Channel Nine News," said Brian over at the main news desk. "Let's send it back to Layla for a little more information about a big storm brewing for next week."

"That's right," said Layla. "We're tracking a warm front coming up from the south that's bringing a lot of moisture. At this point it doesn't look like it will be too severe, but as it develops there is the possibility that we could see some lightning late Tuesday into early Wednesday."

Marty walked over to me again and whispered, "Go behind her again."

Here we go.

I walked around to the edge of the green screen and then came up behind Layla. As soon as I entered the screen, she stopped mid-sentence and turned to me.

"Can we cut? I can't take this anymore." She sounded pissed.

Shit.

"You can't go waving your huge cock around while I'm trying to give the weather."

"Sorry, I..."

"How would you like it if you were trying to give the weather and I started shoving my tits in your face? In fact, why don't you try it." She pointed to the teleprompter.

I started reading. " Rainfall totals should be..."

Next to me, Layla pushed her tits together and licked her lips while staring right at my dick.

"...no more than two or three inches."

Layla dropped to her knees and gripped my shaft in one hand. She pushed it straight up and licked my cock from the base to the tip like it was a lollipop. I looked down and saw that she was looking up at me. I had never seen a girl look so hungry for cock before. She wrapped her lips around it and took it into her mouth. Her hand worked in unison with her soft lips as she bobbed up and down on my cock.

I glanced up and saw that everyone in the studio was watching. Not only that, but the little red light on the camera indicated that millions of people in Miami were also watching. *Every guy in Miami probably wishes Layla was sucking their cock, but she's not. She's sucking mine. And she's loving it.*

Chapter 13
LAYLA

I swirled my tongue around Ethan's huge cock and tasted his pre-cum. He was so ready to fuck me. And I was definitely ready for him to fuck me. My career was probably over. It didn't matter what Marty said. I was pretty sure he would find a reason to fire me if I didn't do this. And I wasn't even sure I wanted to protest. Ethan was sexy. And sweet. And maybe Claire was right. Maybe this would make the National Weather Service notice me. And if it didn't, at least I'd still have my job here.

I didn't care anymore that all my co-workers were watching or that it was being broadcast in HD to the entire city of Miami. I just wanted to have Ethan inside of me. And by the time I was done, every girl in the city was going to wish they were me, and every guy in the city was going to wish they were fucking me.

I pulled my mouth off Ethan and stood up. I was supposed to be saying yes to new opportunities. And all I wanted was to scream yes with him deep inside of me. "Ready to fuck me?"

"Not yet." He grabbed my waist with his muscular arms and flipped me upside down. I spread my legs wide in the air and he leaned in and kissed my clit hard.

Oh God. I returned the favor by wrapping my lips around his cock. Then I imitated every move he made. He flicked his tongue against my clit; I flicked mine across the tip of his cock. He licked in a straight line; I licked his cock up and down. Then he jammed his tongue inside of me. *Yes!* The warmth of his tongue felt incredible, but I wanted him to lick deeper. So I leaned in until his cock started to go down my throat. It made it impossible to breath, but I didn't care. Cock was better than air. Especially when it made Ethan swirl his tongue around deep inside of me.

He spun me back around so that I was standing on the ground. Without hesitation, I turned away from him, put my hands on the floor, and arched my back. *Give me that cock.*

He grabbed my hips with his strong hands and guided his cock inside of me. *Yes!* It felt even better than I had imagined. And he was only half way in. "Keep going," I moaned as he pushed farther and farther in. Then he pulled nearly all the way out and thrust back in. I tried to push back so that he would go deeper, but I couldn't get enough leverage with my hands on the floor.

I pushed him off of me, got to my feet, grabbed his cock, and dragged him over to the news desk. The second I bent over, Ethan's cock was in me again, filling me. I pushed back and felt him go deeper than I even knew was possible.

Brian was sitting a foot away. He took advantage of the opportunity and held a mic to my face.

Is he really going to interview me while I'm being fucked?

The answer was yes.

"So, Layla, how does it feel right now knowing that everyone in the city is watching?" he asked.

Ethan grabbed a handful of my hair and yanked me back onto his cock.

"Harder!" I screamed.

Brian laughed. "I guess that means you're enjoying it."

"Of course I'm enjoying it." I moaned as Ethan's length moved in and out of me.

"Don't you think that what you're doing is a little inappropriate for the news? Children could be watching."

I couldn't help but notice the TV screen in the world news section of the studio. They were preparing to do a segment about ISIS decapitating one of their prisoners, complete with the unedited tape.

"How is me getting fucked worse than that tape of ISIS cutting off a man's head? In fact, maybe what the news needs is more sex and less violence."

"I agree," said Ethan. "In fact, I'll be happy to come back and fuck Layla any time she wants. Maybe that could be a new segment rather than all this depressing crap about houses burning down and people being shot." Ethan thrust into me again and I slammed my hand down onto the desk.

Brian was speechless. He couldn't believe that we would have a moral argument with him while I was bent over his news desk being fucked by a huge cock. Instead of confronting the issue, he decided to go back to trying to embarrass me.

"Is it going to be awkward when you meet people knowing that they've seen you have sex?" asked Brian.

"Why would that be awkward? Everyone has sex." I groaned. Sex had never felt this amazing before. I didn't know if it was because of Ethan's huge cock or all the eyes on me.

"But they've seen that you like sucking dick and being bent over this news desk."

"And I'm sure everyone watching would have enjoyed it just as much as I did. But you know what I'd like even more?"

"No, what?"

"If I had another cock to put in my mouth while Ethan fucks me from behind." I licked my lips and stared at Brian's crotch. Then I reached back, pulled one of Ethan's hands up to my mouth, and started sucking his pointer finger like it was another delicious erection.

Brian couldn't resist the temptation. He immediately unzipped his pants and pulled out his penis. It was way smaller than Ethan's. Maybe five inches.

"Sorry, not big enough." Even if it had been a foot long, I still wasn't going to suck it. But having him pull out his cock on live TV only to be called small was priceless. *At least now I won't be the only one who's embarrassed on live TV.*

Ethan pulled out and pushed on my hips to get me to turn over. I lay back on the news desk and raised my legs high in the air. The glass desk was cold on my naked back. Ethan teased me by grabbing his cock and smacking it against my clit. I was close to orgasm, and he knew it. He pushed his cock deep inside of me and rubbed my clit with his fingers.

"You like that?" he asked.

"Yes!"

"You want it harder?"

"Yes! Fuck, yes."

He went faster and faster, rhythmically rubbing my clit and matching the pace with his thick cock.

"More," I moaned.

He pulled his cock out so that just the tip remained inside of me and then he thrust in deeper and harder than ever before. "FUCK!" I screamed as I lost control of every muscle in my body. My body shook with pleasure and my hands grabbed the edge of the news desk to push myself further down onto Ethan's cock.

Chapter 14
ETHAN

Layla's pussy tightened around me as she orgasmed. Watching her throw her head back and moan as her beautiful body shook was so fucking hot. She tried to get more by grabbing the edge of the news desk and pushing herself towards me, and I wasn't about to stop her. I grabbed her hips and thrust in and out of her as I watched her big tits bounce up and down.

Fuck, I'm going to cum soon.

I pulled out and tried to relax for a second, but Layla wouldn't allow it. She grabbed my cock, dragged me over to the front of the news desk, and pushed me onto the ground. Then she straddled me and lowered herself onto my cock. With her legs wide open, everyone would be able to see every inch of me going into her shaved pussy.

She reached down and played with her clit while she slid up and down the length of my cock. I couldn't take my eyes off her tiny little waist and her perfect tits bouncing up and down.

I sat up and pushed my face between her tits, but she immediately pushed me back down.

"I can't have you blocking everyone's view," she said. "I want everyone in the city to see all eight inches of you going inside me."

Holy shit.

Layla leaned back to give the camera the best view possible. I grabbed her hips and pushed down until I could feel her clit against my skin. I kept her there for a second before loosening my grip. She started bouncing up and down again as soon as she was free.

Then suddenly she stopped and stood up. "I think I need to go finish the weather report now."

"Huh?" *She better not blue ball me on live TV.*

I followed her back to the green screen. I loved watching her round ass move back and forth with every step she took.

She's crazy if she thinks she's going to do the news without me fucking her.

"I'm seeing on the radar that we have a new forecast for this evening," she said. Then she paused and looked at my cock. "Cloudy with a good chance of cum on my face."

Layla dropped down in front of me with her legs wide open. She rubbed her clit with one hand and grabbed the base of my cock with the other. Then she jammed my entire erection into her mouth. No hesitation, no gag reflex. Her nose pressed into my skin and I could feel her tight throat strangling the tip of my cock. She stayed down for a solid five seconds.

Layla started to pull back, but I wasn't done with her yet. I grabbed her hair and thrust into her mouth. She didn't seem to mind at all. When I let go of her hair, she grabbed my hips and made me fuck her beautiful face.

"Fuck, I'm gonna cum," I said.

She pulled back, looked up at me, and opened her mouth wide. Her tongue was sticking out, eager to catch my cum. Both of her hands were squeezing her big tits.

Chapter 15
LAYLA

Ethan reached down and stroked his thick cock. His whole body tensed as white hot cum erupted from his cock. Some of the delicious liquid went in my mouth, but most of it splashed onto my cheeks. There was a momentary pause and then another huge shot of cum filled my mouth. He aimed the next shot at my cheek and then a fourth landed on my neck and tits.

Shit that's a lot of cum.

But he wasn't finished. Cum blasted onto my face and then he finished with another huge shot in my mouth.

I looked up at him as I closed my mouth and swallowed his cum. *Delicious*. But I wanted more. I leaned in and licked the cum off the tip of his cock and then put my lips around it and went down to make sure I didn't miss any. Just for fun I leaned in further and deep throated his massive cock one more time before pulling off.

I glanced at the camera display to see how much cum was on my face. *Holy shit.* I had never seen so much cum. Both my cheeks were covered in it and it was dripping off my chin onto my tits. Ethan was standing over me triumphantly with his huge cock still inches from my face.

I looked over to see if Brian was going to sign off, but he wasn't at the news desk anymore. I figured he must have stomped off after I tricked him into showing everyone his tiny dick.

I decided to seize the opportunity. With cum still dripping from my face, I got up and walked over to take Brian's usual seat.

"I'm Layla Torrez with Channel Nine News. Goodnight, Miami."

Usually Brian played with papers on the desk to look busy while the credits rolled rather than just sitting there awkwardly. There were no papers for me to play with, but I was still covered in cum. I ran my finger across my tits and then licked the cum off of it as the credits rolled.

Marty immediately began clapping as soon as we were off air. Everyone else in the studio followed his lead.

As my horniness began to subside, the realization of what I had just done started to sink in. I had just fucked Ethan and let him cum all over my face. In front of my coworkers. On live TV.

But it had felt amazing. Besides, it was too late to do anything about it now.

Ethan walked up and joined me at the news desk. "Layla, that was incredible," he said. "But I think you still owe me something."

"What could I possibly owe you? You better not ask to do me in the ass."

"No, I just want your phone number."

What's Next?

Layla had one wild afternoon...but that would just be another day for one of my all-time favorite characters - Chastity. She's absolutely wild in the best way possible.

The Single Girl Rules are not your normal boring girl code rules. Do I look like a basic B to you? I mean look at me on that cover totally slaying that dress.

No, these rules are extra AF. And since I'm about to get married...I have to hand them off to the next generation of single girls looking for some steamy guidance. That means you!

Get your copy today!

The Tutor

Weather girls aren't the only ones who get to have fun. Just ask Sophia...She gets crazy right on campus!

Sophia has had a crush on Wyatt ever since they met. Tutoring him at the library once a week has been the highlight of her semester. But their sexual tension is slowly torturing her. Wyatt is sexy, funny, flirtatious, and as far as she can tell - completely unattainable.

When it is time for their last tutoring session, she worries it will be the last time she will ever get to see him. She's determined to not let that happen. Dreaming about him and watching him from a distance at his baseball games isn't going to cut it.
But will she have the confidence to confess her true feelings?

For your free copy, go to:
www.ivysmoak.com/the-tutor-freebie

About the Author

Ivy Smoak is the Wall Street Journal, USA Today, and Amazon #1 bestselling author of *The Hunted Series*. Her books have sold over 2 million copies worldwide.

When she's not writing, you can find Ivy binge watching too many TV shows, taking long walks, playing outside, and generally refusing to act like an adult. She lives with her husband in Delaware.

Facebook: IvySmoakAuthor
Instagram: @IvySmoakAuthor
Goodreads: IvySmoak

Printed in Great Britain
by Amazon